*This book is dedicated to my wife Ann
and our dear friend Pam.
Their invaluable insights moves me forward.
Thank you ladies.*

PATHWAYS
Through
THE FOREST

PALMETTO

P U B L I S H I N G

Charleston, SC

www.PalmettoPublishing.com

Paperback ISBN: 9798822962132

PATHWAYS
Through
THE FOREST

RICHARD BLANEY

Chapter 1

In keeping the spirit and vital soul together,
are you able to maintain their perfect harmony?

- Lao Tzu

Twenty-eight days…

Darkness enveloped the path from the carport to the screened-in back porch. Through the freshly cut grass smoldering in the pitch, a tiny glow from the face of a portable radio guided me onto the cement steps and through the screen door.

"Home already?" my father said.

Unfortunately, I thought.

"Too many people," I said, "I'm tired anyway."

The radio hissed and crackled, the play-by-play fading in and out.

"Four-two in the seventh," he said. "Cincinata's up. Startin' to hit Blass."

"They gonna yank 'im?"

"Pretty soon." A long pause, then he added, "Yep. Pretty soon. I seen some of them fireworks go off. Clear night tonight."

"They were pretty impressive. Too much for me, though. Want a beer?"

"Yeah, get me one."

After fumbling past the milk cartons, chipped ham, and butter, I found a single can of beer. Rather than go downstairs to the cellar to get more, I looked through the bottom cabinet, among the pots and pans, until I found the Irish whiskey I remembered buying a year ago. I poured myself three fingers, thought about it, and then added a couple more and carried it with the cold beer back to the porch.

"You cut the grass," I said as I handed him the beer and settled on the cushioned chaise. "I thought I was going to do it."

"Yeah, well…"

"Everything's so green around here. Did you have a lot of rain this year?"

"Oh yeah, lots of rain. Good garden year." He swallowed beer.

The whiskey was a welcome warmth in my throat. My father wasn't much for conversation unless he really had something to say or if something caught his interest. Otherwise, small talk was not one of his strong points. The whiskey quieted my brain. The crickets and creek frogs seemed to bleep weakly and infrequently in the dark night. I took a hard swallow.

I wondered why I even bothered coming here, to this small, isolated corner of the world where nothing happened and most everybody tried desperately to escape. The Great Depression had never ended in the Laurel Highlands of southwestern Pennsylvania.

"Lots of rain. That's for sure." My father had that way of holding on to a thought, even for an hour or more, and then picking up on it as if there'd been no pause.

"I been up on the mountain cuttin' wood. Seen lots of signs. There's a lot of feed up the mountain. Lotsa feed means lotsa game."

The phone rang in the kitchen. Thinking about another whiskey anyway, I rose.

"Phone's ringing," I announced.

"Is it?" my father said. "Don't let it wake your mother."

I caught it just before it began another ring. "Hello?"

"Hello," replied a feminine voice. "Is this the Flaherty residence?"

"Yes?"

"Is there a…a James R. Flaherty there?"

"Speaking."

"James R. Flaherty? Can you give me your Social Security number?"

"What? Is this somebody I know?" I stretched the phone cord as I poured another shot.

"No," the voice said with a nervous laugh. "I'm sorry. I'm trying to find the owner of this wallet I found."

"Wallet?" I checked my back pocket: empty! "Yeah, it's mine. Oh no! All my money, and my ID. Where did you find it?"

"Social Security number?"

"Oh, 181-24-3622."

"good."

"I was at the fireworks on the Cheat River. I must've dropped it there. I'm in White House, Pennsylvania. Thanks."

"I found it there, on the ground in the parking lot. In fact, I stepped on it."

"Can I pick it up tomorrow? Where are you calling from?"

"I won't be home until the afternoon. I can drop it in the mail."

"I'd rather pick it up myself."

"Well, OK, after one o'clock. Do you know where Pittsburgh Street is in Morgantown?"

"Off 119, from Point Marion?"

"Once you get on Pittsburgh, go four blocks until you come to Cherry. There's a grocery store on the corner. Turn left up a steep hill. It's a brick street. When you get to the top of the hill, you hit Grace. It's a small street with lots of trees. Turn right, second house on the right. It has a green-stripe awning and front door with oval glass."

"Who should I ask for?"

"Just be here at one-thirty, OK?"

"Will do. Listen, thanks, if…"

"One-thirty, Mr. Flaherty. I'm very busy."

"One-thirty it is, then. Goodbye."

"Bye-bye."

Back on the porch, I said, "I dropped my wallet at the fireworks."

"Did you?"

"That was some girl in Morgantown. I'm going to pick it up tomorrow. Want another beer?"

"I'll be damned. Lucky boy, I'll tell ya."

"I know. Anybody could've picked it up. Beer?"

"Nah, that's enough for me. I'm goin' to bed."

"What about the game?"

"Over."

"Who won?"

"Cincinata. Five-four. Good night."

"OK. I'll see ya in the morning."

🌲

I wasn't used to the chilly mornings in the mountains. The mist fell like a heavy frost compared to the warm humidity of Vietnam. I wore a plaid shirt and corduroy jeans.

My father's old VW chugged across the Point Marion bridge with a sputter. Once I came upon the grocery store on the corner of Pittsburgh and Cherry, I wondered if the Bug could make the steep cobblestone hill onto which it was directed, but the old VW was equal to the challenge.

I knew by now that Grace Street led straight into West Virginia University's campus, via the Mountaineer Stadium; this young lady must be a student. Two very large sycamores shaded the house so that little sunlight reached the street. Through a passing shiver that left goose bumps, I stepped up to the heavy oak door with the beveled oval window and knocked.

A moment later, the old door cracked ajar before swinging halfway open. A young woman emerged. She wore a hopsack-looking dress that almost touched the floor; it was off-white with dark-blue seams, Indian in design. It perfectly set off her deeply tanned neck and face and chestnut hair, which lay on her shoulders. I noticed her green eyes at her second glance.

"Are you James?"

"Jimmy." I liked the husky quality of her voice.

"Let me get your wallet," she said without inviting me in. When she returned with it, she tossed her head to one side, her hair now behind her shoulder. "Here it is."

"I don't know how to thank you. All my papers, ID, and money are in this wallet."

"Twelve hundred and seventy-four dollars. I know." Her green eyes twinkled a bit.

She cocked her head slightly. "Are you a soldier or something?"

"On leave. If I'd lost this wallet, I'd be in for a worse time than I expect to have anyway."

She looked at me curiously. "I thought soldiers had short hair and, well, no mustache or beard or anything."

"They usually don't," I laughed.

"Are you on leave from Vietnam?" she asked abruptly.

"Can't you tell from these clothes?" I replied, looking down at my corduroys. "I haven't adjusted to this climate yet."

"Oh. Well, I'm glad I found your wallet and your money."

"Is there some way I can repay you? Anything?"

"That won't be necessary." She started to close the door.

"Maybe." I touched the door. "Maybe you'll let me treat you to dinner?"

Her face wrinkled. "No, I don't think that would be possible."

"It's just that"—my hand still extended—"I have a month with really nothing to do, and, well, it's been a long time…"

"A long time?" she replied.

"That's not what I meant to say."

"Whatever it is, it's OK." Her eyes cooled.

I drew my hand back, face stinging with a blush, and there followed an uncomfortable silence. My face must've appeared stone still, for she relented a bit with her expression. With that, I withdrew.

"Well, thanks again," I said and turned quickly.

As I reached the sidewalk, she called out, "Were you in the fighting?"

What an odd question, I thought. But I answered without turning my head, "Was, but not anymore."

"But you're going back there? What do you do?"

I turned. She was holding on to the door.

"I work in MACV now. I'm fine."

"MACV?"

"Pacification and Vietnamization, if you can believe it's possible."

"That must be interesting." She hadn't moved.

"It kills the time. That's about all I can say about it."

I turned again, walked around the VW, and opened the door.

"Goodbye, Mr. Flaherty, James R.," she said, resting her head on her arm.

Even at that distance, and in the dark shade of the trees, I could make out her smile.

I forced a grin and shook my head. I waved quickly, got in the Bug, and drove away.

Chapter 2

Twenty-four days.......

"Glad you're back, Jimmy," said Audie.

"Just a month," I replied.

"Goin' back there?" Georgie gaped. "You're not right in the head!"

Audie squirted amber speetle through his teeth. "She-e-i-t. You're whipped."

"I ain't whipped," I snapped back.

"Whippo."

"Whippo," Georgie repeated. "You'd think you had enough, jag-off."

"Don't call me that."

"Jag-off!"

We carried long-handled baskets up the mountain.

"Sutton Flats," I said. "Best place for blackberries."

"Black bears, too," returned Georgie.

Turning and spitting into the brush, Audie said, "I ain't seen bear in years." His dirt-stained freckles appeared like he just came out of a coal mine.

I couldn't help but say, "You look silly. That chew makes you look like a chipmunk."

Audie defiantly forced out another. His blue eyes shot a stern look.

Georgie warned, "I hope we don't run into any copperheads!"

They were out now. They liked to rest on rocks and under fallen tree trunks, where we were now making our way through jaggers and mountain laurel. Georgie's face was streaked with sweat over his chubby cheeks, and my hair lay in wet strands on the back of my neck. Audie spit out his chew and flung it over fallen timber.

"Look out!" cried Georgie. "You stirred up that copperhead there."

Audie's spent chew nearly landed on the snake. It reared and twisted but didn't need to defend itself so it slid away. We braced ourselves after the scare.

"Whew, that was damn close!" Audie said.

"OK, we ain't hurt. Let's get to them blackberries." Audie spit out another flake.

We had to half crawl, clinging to ferns and long, flat shale boulders. It was worth the struggle, though, and we found the blackberry bushes. The thorniest ones had the best fruit, and we surrounded them. An hour later, our fingers and hands scratched and itching, our baskets were filled. The leaves rustled in a slight breeze.

Audie said, "My mom makes the best cobbler on earth. I can't wait."

"With ice cream," Georgie added.

Audie tore off another chew. His right cheek bulged before his first spit ejected like a spray hose. Georgie squinted.

I said, "I met a college girl couple days ago."

"Was she pretty?"

"Very."

Audie spit and asked, "How'd you meet her?"

"I lost my wallet down at Cheat Lake. She called next morning that she found it. I drove down to Morgantown. She even told me how much money I carried."

"Lucky," Georgie said.

"I know. Anybody else would've kept it."

"You make a move?" Amber juice landed close to my toe.

"Yeah, but she blew me off."

Audie said, "Buh God, I'll tell you one damn thing. I wouldn't let that happen to me."

I picked up my basket. "Let's get off this mountain."

I went first, through chokeweed that gradually thickened. Honey locust bent with the breeze, and laurel and wild grapes perfumed it. The forest darkened into quiet, shadowy waves as their voices were farther behind me. I came across layers of large shale and stepped gingerly sideways and downward. Almost slipping, I held the basket and strained to balance. I spilled a few berries but righted the basket. I decided to rest on a shale rock. I caught my breath, sighed, and glanced around. The forest had swallowed me. Now I blinked. I was alone. Where did they go? I must've turned the wrong way and might end up on the Cheat River! Panicked, I thrashed my way downward. Suddenly I was parting through jaggers and nipa palm. Coconut trees towered over the lemon blossoms, and the nipa fans whipped, crackling, in the fierce wind. The canals gushed from the new tide, and the river rippled toward me. I slid into the mud, and the berries spilled. I squashed until blood rolled on the rocks. A cobra reared and hissed, and I fell on my side, past the crabs oozing away. I saw rice stalks and grabbed. I pulled myself onto the rice field and sank to my knees.

"Jimmy! What are you doin' in that puddle?" It was Georgie.

"Got lost," I answered. "Where'd you guys go?"

"Yonder and yonder." Audie pointed.

"Well, guys," I said, " time to go."

"Good seein' ya again, Jimmy boy," Georgie said.

"Yeah," Audie said. "When're we going to see you again?"

Never, I thought. You live in a created reality. I live in the real world, although one that's a "surd reality" like a vacuum without reason. Insecure chaos. No, we'll never come together again.

"See you guys," I lied.

I wonder what Mom will say when I return home without the blackberries?

Two days later, I was pulling weeds in the garden, considering a trip the next morning to Pittsburgh. I figured on going to a ball game after dinner at an Italian place I liked, then maybe doing some clubbing on the Diamond. I could get a hotel room at the Hilton, sort of a R&R-type splurge, and then go out to the museums in Oakland the next day. I had always enjoyed the museum of natural history and the art museum. I read that an Irish art collection was on display.

My mother called from the kitchen window, "Jimmy!"

"Yeah?"

"Phone!"

Phone? Nobody knows I'm home, at least nobody I'd want to see who was still in the area. "I'll be right there."

"It's a girl," my mother said. I could tell she was curious. "You expectin' to hear from someone?"

"Not really. Did she say who she was?"

"You better get it."

My father sat at the table looking at me when I picked up the receiver. "Hello?"

"Mr. Flaherty, James R.?"

I recognized her voice and felt my heart race a bit. "Yeah," I said meekly.

"Would you consider going to a discussion group with me?"

"A discussion group?"

"It's a group of friends. We get together once a week…"

"What do you discuss?"

She laughed nervously. "Anything that seems current. It's really just a social gathering more than anything. You know, pitchers of beer and moralizing." She laughed again.

"Well, sure, I guess."

"I think you'll find it interesting, and…it will break the monotony of your boring leave time."

"Where should I go?"

"Just come by the house and get me. About six or so. We can walk to it from here."

"About six, then," I said. "I'll see you then."

Chapter 3

Twenty-one days.....

She greeted me at the door, green eyes bright. She wore jeans and a white blouse with epaulettes, the sleeves rolled up. Her hair waved around her face, and I noticed how unblemished and smooth her skin was. Her eyebrows were as thick as her hair, her nose small and round, delicate-looking, and her lips blushed naturally and fully. When she smiled at my arrival, dimples formed on each cheek.

The smile was at my plaid shirt again. I looked at myself and shrugged, "Still cold."

"Let's go, Flaherty, James R."

"Jimmy," I corrected, "and listen, I don't even know your name."

"Diana," she answered.

"Diana," I said, trailing off, waiting for the rest.

"Last names aren't important," she said then, "but it's Levin."

"I was really surprised when you called," I said. "I thought I'd never see you again."

"I'm known for my surprises."

We walked two blocks down Grace and then cut right, down another steep hill. Halfway down, she led me into a narrow side street, almost an alley. We continued for half a block until we reached a bar with no name. It just had a red neon "Beer-Wines-Liquor" sign. Crosby, Stills, and Nash were on the stereo inside. The wooden floor was uneven and creaky. The place reminded me of an old grocery store; maybe it was the sawdust on the floor causing me some unsteady steps through the smoky, stale-beer semidarkness. We reached a large, solitary table in the back, lit with metallic haze under a black light.

The seven people at the table, two women and five men, seemed to glow. Buttons, belt buckles, jewelry, and even beer foam glowed while eyes and noses remained dark and mysterious until my eyes adjusted to the light.

An older man, half bald with a thick handlebar mustache and goatee spoke up first. "Ah, Diana, how are you tonight?"

"I brought you a special guest," she answered cheerily, "and a new friend. James"—she glanced at me—"Flaherty." She pointed in turn, first to the man who greeted her. "Allan Dalton, professor of English; Ginny Malheim, classmate and friend; Marilyn Springs; John Mayhew; Walen Sturdivant, a.k.a. 'Whale-Turd.'"

"Ah, yes," said the professor, holding up his half-drunk beer, "The Whale-Turd!"

Diana laughed. "And this is my friend Dwight, and over there sits Richard, brooding with insight."

Whale-Turd, appropriately enough, was fat. Ginny was big and chunky, with a friendly smile. Marilyn was blond, with long legs that poured from her baggy khaki shorts, and Richard sat with his brown hair parted in the middle, a slightly pocked face, hard and worn. But Dwight caught my attention.

He seemed to bristle at me. He had dark-blond, curly hair that bushed wildly and round glasses held in place by gold wire frames that still glowed in the black light. "Get yourself a glass," he said, with an underlying tone of demand.

The professor poured Diana and me glasses of beer and called for another pitcher. He said, "We were discussing Emily Dickinson's imagery when you came in."

"You got here just in time!" Ginny chuckled.

Dwight held the chair next to him for Diana, with an authoritative gesture. I sat next to the professor, which was fortunate because Marilyn's legs were in full view from there.

"So, James," asked Whale-Turd, "what's your major?"

"Well—"

"James is on leave from Vietnam," interrupted Diana.

"Oh?" The professor straightened. "A warrior home for a well-deserved rest?"

"Not exactly," I said.

"Are we really pulling out as much as Nixon says we are?" asked Richard in a deep voice.

"Yes, I think so."

"You think so?" It was Dwight. "You were there. If you don't know, how can we believe it's true?"

"When I said 'I think so,' that's just what I meant: I think so. Troop reduction is not gauged by pullouts as much as a reduction in replacements. To the best of my knowledge, very few replacements are coming in-country."

"The numbers game," said the professor. "We've been so swamped with numbers and statistics for the past five years, it's no wonder we're always in a state of confusion."

"And five years *for what*?" Dwight snapped. "We still have the draft, and ROTC still recruits right on our campus."

Dwight's arm reached across Diana's chair, almost embracing her. His round glasses reflected the pale light as he spoke. "As far as I'm concerned, the whole mess is an affront to human decency." His voice was rising. "And furthermore, no person of true conscience would be there."

"That's a bit extreme," I countered. "Don't you think? After all, there're a lot of decent, good people there, who want to be there, with a sense of purpose. If for nothing else but to judge for themselves what's going on."

"Meaning no one can speak out unless they've been there?"

"Meaning," I replied, "one's opinion should reflect some depth." I shifted uncomfortably in my chair and swallowed the rest of the beer in my glass.

The professor immediately poured me another. "Gentlemen, we shouldn't waste our time with recrimination. We have an opportunity here. Let's not waste it for any personal…reasons." He glanced at Diana.

I said, "The professor's right. I can't answer for our government or policy-makers, but I can give an informed opinion based on my experience. And I'll tell you another thing, very few of the guys over there would disagree with Dwight."

"One thing that's always bothered me," said Ginny, "is how anyone can doubt the rightness of the war and yet go right out and be part of it. It seems to me if you don't believe in it, you should go to Canada or Sweden rather than commit the atrocities that perpetuate it."

The professor said, "What do you think, Marilyn? You've been quiet tonight."

"I don't like talking about it," she said softly. "I'm just, well, tired of it all."

An impasse of sorts followed, the members of the group assessing each other.

Dwight leaned closer to Diana and gave her a quick hug. She responded, "Marilyn is right. Do any of you realize how long it's been since any of us talked about the war, like we used to? We're about to graduate soon, maybe that's why. But I remember when we were all active. You, too, Marilyn. Weren't you first arrested for demonstrating in opposition to Cambodia? And Dwight was an inspiring student leader then, coordinating and planning with others at other campuses. What's happened to our commitment? Our passion?"

"If I may say so," I said, "I think it's because you've been effective in your opposition."

After another pause, the professor said, "Well, are we going to hash this out or leave it again?"

"I think we should," Richard's rich voice said, "at least for old times' sake."

"It's true," said Ginny. "Maybe we've won and don't realize it. But I'd still like an answer to my question. James?"

I felt a little strange then. This really wasn't my world, and I didn't relish the role of defender of the faith. I said, "Look, I could go into it in detail, but it'd be a long story, and I might not express it in words to do it justice."

"It seems to me," the professor answered, "we have all the time in the world. Let's get another pitcher."

"Yes, Jimmy," Diana added, her eyes fixed on me, "I'd like to hear what you think."

Dwight heaved a sigh. "At least it means a few more beers."

I began to smooth my mustache. I'd gotten into something quite different from what I had expected, and now I felt trapped. I looked around the table, at each face.

"I'd have to say first that each of you is far beyond where I should be. In a year or so from now, I'll be just starting out in school, where you will have graduated and launched your careers. I'm envious, but as I sit here and listen, I realize that my time hasn't been completely wasted. How? I can't say. It's just a feeling.

"The war, to me, has three distinct stages. The first from, '65 to the Tet Offensive in '68, then the lull until Cambodia in '70, and now this current stage, the end as far as we're concerned. Sure, we were involved as early as the fifties and in force from '61, but as far as general America is concerned, '65 started it all.

"Now, Mr. Nixon's promise with his quote-unquote plan has decidedly changed the tenor of the conflict. This, I think, is the most dangerous situation for the GIs, because Cambodia changed everything, and I know because I was there to witness the decline in morale and thinking."

"What effect do you think Kent State had for the soldiers?" the professor asked.

"A very powerful one, Allan. Strong enough to change everything, which really comes to the answer of Ginny's question."

"Then I'd like to see the connection," said Ginny.

"How does all this connect," snapped Dwight, "with the morality of it all?"

"Wait a minute, Dwight." It was Marilyn. She pulled her legs under her chair and sat up straight. "Let the man tell his story." She sipped some beer and seemed to relax, and her legs slowly extended and crossed at the ankles.

I sighed ever so slightly at the sight of her legs again. "I'm just trying to set the overall stage, the grand drama of it all. Now we're a defeated army, withdrawing with as much dignity as we can keep, under the shield of Mr. Nixon's quote-unquote 'Pacification/Vietnamization' program. But what about us, the GI, the regular American, caught in the middle of that mess? At the risk of sounding like Dwight here, casuistic, I'd like to express in the best words I can how we feel…how we live in this…this morass."

Dwight stiffened. "Casuistic?"

"A disingenuous reasoner"—the professor winked—"especially in questions of morality."

He raised his beer glass to me in salute.

I began to feel better now; the beer had washed away my inhibitions, and I was proud of the thrust at Dwight. Diana chuckled at it but also noticed my eyes had returned to Marilyn's legs. I caught her quick glance, thinking, *What the hell? Why not let it loose and pour out everything I'd been holding inside?* I'd been set up by Diana, I realized now. Dwight went for it, and that was his problem. I, James Flaherty, was not about to be part of that game. I washed down the rest of the beer and belched—at which Whale-Turd cheerily approved.

"Even as we sit here, drinking beer, listening to music, enjoying each other's company, young men are waking—it's before dawn over there—shivering cold and wet. Probably after little sleep, two or three hours at the most, boiling water for powdered coffee, opening cans of C rations for a breakfast of cold ham and lima beans. Who are these men? What do they think? Well, odds are they've either graduated from college or have dropped out for one reason or another. The days of the blue-collar soldier have given way to the more educated, drafted soldier, as well as the company officer right out of ROTC.

"They'd probably close in on your naive, inexperienced faces and say, 'Wait a minute! You're all wrong. Not in what you hope to accomplish, but in the way you do it, and who you do it to!'

"For you see, and you too, Professor, the things you see on your TV screen aren't always what they appear to be."

"What the hell does that mean?" Dwight blustered.

"Means, Dwight, that I am damn glad that your passion and commitments are gone! How could we possibly survive any more of it, you and I?"

"You…" stumbled Dwight, "and I?"

I flashed a glance at Diana and then nodded to Dwight. "That's right, Dwight. You and I. But in one minute, just you, for I'm leaving now."

"No reason to hurry." The professor tried to calm the situation as I rose to leave. "We have more beer on the way and hopefully some more lively conversation."

"Thanks, Professor, but the game's over for me now." I bowed courteously to the group. I looked at Diana. "Can I see you a minute?"

"Why are you leaving?" she asked.

We had gone to the end of the bar right in front of the door, "Country Roads" playing from the stereo. "You're not letting Dwight chase you away, are you?"

"I don't appreciate being used."

"Used?"

"C'mon, Diana, I know what you're up to."

"Whatever Dwight says or does," she replied sharply, "is strictly how Dwight and no one else feels. He speaks for himself and himself only."

"Then, what's between you two has no bearing on it?"

"There is nothing, I mean nothing, between us except a friendship we've shared since junior high up in Pittsburgh."

"I don't think that's how he sees it, as if you really didn't know."

She shook her head. "You have this all wrong, James. A total misconception from…"

"What did you call me?"

"What?"

"Just now, what did you call me?"

"James?"

"First time you used my name."

"You mean your first name? Have you forgotten I introduced you as James?"

"But this is the first time you said my name naturally."

"What's it got to do with…" She gestured toward the group's table.

"Don't you see? Progress. Maybe even the beginning of the end of you and Dwight." I smiled.

"Oh! I'll tell you one more time, maybe the last time…"

"It definitely will be the last time! I'm leaving." And I walked out.

♣

Commandeering the old Volkswagen over the dark narrow roads after sharing in two or three pitchers of beer mustered all the prowess I had. Whenever the paint of the center line faded into the darkness, I guided the car with sobering terror. My brake foot became heavy with tension, my clutch foot with hyper-anxiety. Finally I swerved the corner at the White House Borough sign, made the sharp bend with enough room [fortunately no cars coming from the Fairchance way] to make it to the dirt driveway without stopping to back up; pretty good handling, I thought.

"Jimmy!" his mother greeted him. "Phone's been ringing 'bout every five minutes. Every time your dad and me pick it up, whoever's on the other side won't answer. Just hangs up. You expectin' a call or somethin'?"

"Sorry, Ma. I'll get it next time."

"Good. I'm tryin' to sleep. It's way past my bedtime."

I regretted volunteering for the phone. The room was slowly spinning. How much beer did I have, anyway? Must've been too much, and the old floral wallpaper didn't help, blending into a patterned gyro with every reel. The ringing phone alerted me.

"Hello?" I picked up the receiver.

"Oh, good," answered Diana, "it's you at last."

"Yeah, it's late."

"You're right, I shouldn't have done that. I'm sorry, James."

I heard Cream in the background.

"But you have to understand, my intentions were much different, believe me."

The song playing, appropriately enough, was "Strange Brew."

"Are you still in that bar?"

"Will you accept my apology?"

"Yeah, sure. You must be drunk, at least I feel that way, and I left over an hour ago."

"I'm fine. Going home now."

"Guess I'm not used to it."

"I'm glad you accepted my apology. I was worried."

"You oughta worry about going home. Maybe Dwight can take you."

"Ha, nice try, but he left."

"Nice boyfriend he is, leaving you at the bar."

"Ya know," she snapped. "You're such a…"

"A smart ass?"

"Yeah, that's it. Goodbye!"

Click!

The phone rang again. "Hello."

"Don't forget, James, you owe me a dinner!"

"Does that mean I'm right about the progress?"

"Means I'm gonna score a good meal tomorrow night. At seven."

Click!

At seven o'clock, the summer sun cast a golden glow through the sycamores in front of her house. I was beginning to get used to the cool mountain air and even wore a short-sleeved shirt for our date.

Diana came to the door smelling of fresh cologne. She wore jeans, a bit faded compared to mine, and very snug. But her shirt was an army one, long-sleeved and khaki with patches and chevrons, as if she were a soldier on pass instead of a pretty student.

"I don't know whether to say hi or salute," I said.

She touched my arm. "Can that old car make it up the mountain?"

"That's a Bug, 'course it can!"

"Good. That's where we're going, for a big steak."

We ended up well into Pennsylvania, near Route 40, at a rustic old inn of logs and pitch that served steaks and seafood. I liked the wide planks of the old wood floor and the tables and chairs fashioned from tree trunks and heavy boughs. Despite the restaurant's remoteness, quite a few people crowded around the salad bar, pecking and poking for the perfect piece of lettuce, I supposed. We were shown to a table for two next to a wall that held old prints of hilly farmland.

She ordered a Bloody Mary, and I chose a whiskey.

"How can you drink that stuff without anything to mix it into?"

I shrugged and enjoyed a first sip. "How did you learn about this place?"

She thought a moment.

I said, "I know. I bet—"

"If you're going to say what I think you're going to say, then don't."

"What's that?" I feigned innocence.

"Despite what you might think, what I said is the truth. Dwight and I really do go back to junior high."

"He likes you."

"And I like him. A good friend."

"No, I mean he likes you as in romance."

"I disagree."

"At least he likes to think he owns you."

"Nobody has that privilege. I think what you see is Dwight the suitor, not Dwight the big brother."

"Sometimes that friendship stuff sneaks up on you."

"Yeah, well…" Her voice trailed off. We looked around the restaurant, quietly musing and sipping our drinks.

"Why don't you go get a salad?"

I watched her navigate from the chopped lettuce to the dressings. The salad bar lights created a halo around her hair, and I liked the way she laughed after a brief tangle between a cherry tomato and the tongs. The tomato escaped the tongs until she picked it up with her fingers and, instead of dropping it onto her plate, popped it into her mouth.

When she returned to the table, I smiled. "That tomato tripped you out."

"Did you see that?" She laughed. "I thought I was going to lose it again!"

"So tell me," she said, picking at her salad, "how did you like our little discussion group?"

Her eyes betrayed the nonchalance her chewing was supposed to convey.

"Oh, I don't know. It was pretty much foreign to me," I replied.

"There was a lot of passion in your voice when you spoke up."

"Too much beer."

"You're blushing." She reached over and stroked my cheek. My skin warmed from her touch. "Aren't you going to get some salad?"

When I got back and sat down, she had pushed away her salad plate and after sipping the rest of the Bloody Mary, said, "You know, I feel comfortable with you. Can I get another?"

Shortly after, the steaks arrived with the accompaniments and were as good as we both were expecting.

"I don't know what it is." She frowned after half of the second drink. "Maybe I shouldn't try to understand."

"Maybe we should just focus on now, while it lasts."

"That's what worries me."

"Don't worry about it. You're just scoring a good meal, remember?"

Through a couple more good meals, I learned that Diana was a senior majoring in history. I also learned that she was a good student, gifted in some areas, with a 3.85 grade point average won from honest effort.

"I believe most of a student's education," she said during a drive, "is in the interactions of the university experience."

We'd gone the thirty-five miles to Kingwood for buckwheat pancakes and sausage at a place I knew about. Afterward, on the way back, she said, "That was delicious," and leaned closer to me as I drove.

"Yeah," I replied. "It's been a long time since I had buckwheat pancakes. Glad I remembered. Glad you enjoyed it."

She patted my shoulder and then ran her fingers down my arm. "In fact, it's all been very good."

"Yeah." I smiled. "Do you like fishing?"

"You've been good for me, James. I feel so relaxed now. I never realized how intense I've been lately."

"Sounds pretty much like the way I've been living these past couple of years," I said. "It's too bad I have to return home, uh, I mean, to leave pretty soon."

Diana fell silent the rest of the way back to Morgantown. She stared out the window, and I saw no need to interrupt her.

She finally said, "Yes, I'd like to go fishing. Where?"

Chapter 4

Eighteen days…

It was 4:00 a.m., and my father helped me load the VW. He had changed the oil and tuned it. I wanted to get there before full sun. An hour and a half away, we could make it if the VW ran well.

Diana came to the door wearing shorts.

I worried. "Do you have long pants? The bugs might be bad."

"I'll be fine."

"I have some repellent just in case, the high-DEET military brand."

"I'll be fine," she said again.

We went south on I-79 to Sutton and turned off onto the Mountaineer Expressway. We continued down past Birch River and up Mount Powell until we reached the plateau of Nicholas County. The low sun shone through the woods as we passed into Fayette County onto Summersville Lake on the Gauley River. After arriving there, we carried our gear under tall oaks, pines, hemlocks, and willows as we made our way down the path to the lake. Black-eyed Susans stared from an open spot. I pulled night crawlers from my cooler, and we hooked the squirmy creatures and cast into the clear green water. Diana's eyes sparkled from the reflection.

She turned to me and smiled. "I realize how blue your eyes are."

"Clear green water," I returned. "Feel anything?"

Gazing into me, she said, "I think so…I mean…"

"Fish?"

"Oh, that. Not yet. How 'bout you?"

She checked her line and reeled in. I checked the bait and replaced a worm, and she threw a long cast. The air warming, she leaned back onto the folded jacket covering the tackle box and covered her eyes. "It's so peaceful and comfortable. I might drift off."

"Dawn and dusk," I said. "My favorites. Fetching."

A while later, the water still calm and quiet, she sat up, looked at her line again, and turned to me. "James, what did your dad do?"

"Coal miner."

"How long?"

"Thirty years or so. He thought he was getting black lung and decided to retire."

"Is he OK?"

"As far as I can see. He's sturdy. Runs in the family."

"Are you?"

"I think so. I'm alive, ain't I?"

"You certainly are!"

We fell back into our fishing. Not much action—a nibble here and there. I cast often but with no luck. Sighing, I asked her, "What does your father do?"

"An attorney. He and my mother practice in his firm. He likes real estate, and she likes labor law."

"I never met an attorney's daughter."

"I applied at Duquesne law. I want to practice labor law as well. I never met a coal miner's son before."

The sun was well up and the air warm, but the fish weren't interested in what we were offering or were further upriver. We moved a few yards up and down the bank, but an hour later, she yanked her line.

"I've had enough. I'm hungry."

I agreed. "Let's go then. There's a place in Fairmont I'd like to stop."

"What kind?"

"Sicilian."

"I'd like that," Diana said.

The Tygert Valley River extruded grumpily below Muriela's, its brown water smelling of fish in stages of decay.

"Whew!" She coughed, fanning her face. "I'm sure glad we didn't catch any fish at the lake."

"I hope there's none from here on the menu," I replied.

We found a nice booth in the corner and took turns washing up.

Returning to her seat, she said, "I didn't realize how hungry I am."

"Fresh air," I returned. "I'm famished, too. What would you like?"

"I love lasagna. But look at the meatballs and marinara. I'll have that, too."

"That's a lot of food, girl. I'm going to have Italian sausage and some linguini with red clam sauce. Like some wine?"

"Oh yes. Barola."

"Expensive?"

"Tasty."

The waitress brought us a basket of hot breads and two glasses of the clear red Italian.

Diana asked for olive oil and then sloshed and sopped the bread. I followed suit and appreciated it it more. We were enjoying the wine and asked for more bread when the food came in several plates. We gorged.

"Can I get you something else?" the waitress asked as she took up the plates.

"Tiramisu." It was Diana.

"Damn, girl. Are you sure?"

"Love it," came the reply.

I paid, and we stumbled out the door.

Diana held her stomach and said, "I won't have to eat for two more days."

"Damn, I need a nap. How about you?"

We looked for the car in the now full parking lot. "I can't remember…"

"James, a VW?"

Once we found it, I groped for the door handle. When I finally opened the door for her, she fell in.

I crunched in my side. "Too much wine," I declared.

"Want me to drive?"

"No, no. I can make it to that motel over yonder," I said, seeing the collection of buildings across the highway.

We checked in, and I asked the clerk for a wakeup call at 6:30 p.m. We settled in.

Diana slurred, "James, am I your escort?"

"I guess in a way."

"I want you to know I like being your escort." She sprawled on her back, and minutes later, she softly snored. I curled up into the fetal position and conked out.

"James, James, time to get up; just answered the call."

I stretched and brushed her bare thigh. "What time is it?"

"Nearly seven." She touched my arm. "We better get a move on."

Refreshed and sober, we drove to Morgantown and her house. I sat on the railing of her front porch as the sycamores cooled the air. Cicadas rattled from the darkness. I remembered our day, the fresh air and summer wildflowers. The water had been so clear, as if it had been through a purifier. The food capped everything, and our nap refreshed us. I liked Diana. She made me feel good about myself again. She was earthy, honest, and innocent, but I had to check myself. In less than a month, she would be on her way to a law career, and I would be back to my old world: destruction and violence.

She appeared in the doorway. "You cold again? You'll get used to here soon."

Not enough time, I thought. I held my hands under my armpits and tapped my feet. She handed me a gray sweater and sat on the porch glider. She asked me to sit with her.

"Slow motion relaxes me," she said.

"Me too."

"Ja-Jimmy, you mind if I ask you about the war?"

"I don't think so. What do you want to know?"

She sat straight and fixed her eyes. "What does—or did it feel like?"

"Hard question," I replied. "Explaining…"

She took my wrist. "You don't have to tell me."

"No, I'd like to. I probably need to tell somebody what I feel. It's hard, I know, but I have to tell someone."

Diana squeezed gently.

"You get taken away," I began, "from everything you know, everyone you know. Your world gone. They put you with strangers and train you to kill. That's all it is. Your world turns upside down. Your morality is stained. You don't know what to believe; you lost your world, you lost your family, you lost your friends. You've become part of a new brotherhood that depends on loyalty. It's all that is left; loyalty and survival is your new world. No escape. You live in a new reality that'll never go away, and you might even kill yourself to return to the old reality. What an irony: kill yourself to find your old world, and nobody cares."

"I care," she said. "I care. Why do people kill for a patch of ground, an idea, a religion, and, worse, national pride? I care." She hugged me and kissed my cheek. "I care."

We fell silent and moved the glider into a gentle sway.

I said, "Now that we're loafin' next couple of weeks, where do you want to go next?"

"Let me think about it."

"I better go home and sleep. Call?"

"Call."

♣

Diana called the next afternoon. "Jimmy, would you like to join me? I'm going to Pittsburgh tomorrow morning."

"Sure."

"I need to visit my family and prepare for my next move."

"I'll join you," I answered.

She arrived in a Ford Pinto. She was wearing overalls, a long-sleeve green and black striped shirt, and a light-green beret. I wore cords, a long-sleeve shirt, and the gray sweater from the afternoon before.

"Still not acclimated?" She smiled. The car started, she backed out of the driveway, and we settled for the drive.

I said, "I'm not surprised you have a Pinto."

"You're not surprised I have a pinto? I always drove a VW Beetle. I thought the Pinto would be a nice change. I like it."

"What are we going to do in Pittsburgh? Besides you visiting your family, I mean."

"You could join me, if you wish."

"Inappropriate. We haven't known each other long enough."

"I'm sure they'd like you."

"Maybe."

Heavy clouds rolled over us as we headed north. The highway rolled past. "Where does your family live?" I asked her.

"Squirrel Hill."

"Where's that?"

She smiled, making he cheek dimples appear. "Out the eastern side of the city."

"I think I'll go to Diamond Square. Can you come back for me?"

"If you want to get home." She laughed, leaned over, and kissed my cheek.

After going through the tunnel and over the river, she pulled the car into a bus lane, and I hopped out. We waved, and she pulled into light traffic heading east. Diamond Square held a five-and-dime store, Klein's Restaurant, The Fish House, and a couple of seedy bars. I chose The Fish House, where I could down some oysters early in the day, with a draft beer. There were no tables, but a long bar was populated by suited businessmen enjoying fish sandwiches. The oysters came in those tiny cups, as if I were getting medicine in the hospital. I slurped and sipped, slurped and sipped, until I had finished two orders. Then I left.

The square teamed with life now. A gathering surrounded the bandstand featuring the Pittsburgh Steelers. Black and gold adorned everything, adding to the festive music and public announcements blaring from a loudspeaker. People milled about, chatting and laughing, surrounded by the cicada-like rhythm of polka music and the smell of grilling kielbasa. I decided to roam and enjoyed the energy and friendliness of the people inside the department stores and along the sidewalks. I found a park bench and relaxed. I wondered when Diana would return. The sun was still fairly high; it was mid-July so it would be near three o'clock. I strolled until I reached one of the shaded corners and then walked back toward the square.

"Jimmy!"

Diana came up smiling and took my arm. "Let's go!"

"Where?"

"Klein's. They serve lobster. You like lobster?"

"Never had it."

"You have a treat in store."

I said, "We're having lobster then."

We crossed a couple of streets with the walking lights toward the north side of the point and entered the restaurant through heavy oak doors along with others coming in for early supper. The brown-and-cream-colored atmosphere reminded me of my parents' style. Once we were seated, she pointed out her favorites on the menu while we waited for service.

"This place makes excellent clam chowder. I'm having that with a small salad before the lobster. You?"

"Lead the way. I'll be trusting you on this one."

After she ordered for both of us and some talk about her afternoon and what I had seen downtown, the food appeared. The aroma was inviting, and I carefully spooned up some of the hot, thick liquid.

"James, dip your spoon away from you."

"Why?"

"You won't spill it on yourself. See?"

"Thanks for the etiquette lesson."

"Practicality. Isn't it good?"

"Any other lessons?"

She smiled, handing me a narrow bottle. "Vinaigrette."

"What?"

"For your salad. Vinegar is good for you."

"How do you know all this?"

"My parents."

"Mine never taught me that."

She laughed. "You're just a country boy!"

"Make you think less of me?"

"It's charming. Here they come."

The lobsters came with small forks, claw crackers, and pick-like utensils.

"What'll I do with these?"

"I'll show you." She tore out the claw and cracked it open. With the pick, she extracted the meat and ate it. I followed her example. The other claw she opened, and juice squirted on her lips and cheek. She chuckled and ate. The tail had already been split. "I love the tail the most. More meat, sweet and juicy."

"Now I can deal with that," I agreed.

As we were finishing our work on the lobsters, she added, "We have a special dessert coming: Hungarian floating cake."

"Why Hungarian?"

"When Klein's first opened, they served kosher and Hungarian dishes."

"But this a seafood restaurant."

Diana pursed her lips into a grin. "Originally kosher but now seafood. Many Catholics come in now."

"Uh?"

"Fish. They eat fish on Fridays. This place rocks during Lent."

"How do you know about all this? Religion, I mean."

She shrugged her shoulders. "James, I like you. Gettin' to know you is a joy. And I've had such a good time."

"Same here, Diana. I'm especially glad I met you. You've filled my time with fun."

"Yeah! A lost wallet. Go figure."

"I wish I were here for good. We could spend more time together."

"If only possible. Here comes my dessert."

I saw what looked like a large eclair floating in heavy cream. Diana poked it and turned the cream over with her spoon. "Crème Anglaise! I love this. Try?"

"Too sweet. The only sweet I like is canned peaches."

Taking in the Anglaise first, her lips surrounded the spoon. She swallowed and closed her eyes. Then she held the spoon to her lips and said, "Sure?"

"Enjoy," I answered.

The next spoonful went in more slowly. The crème oozed onto her lips and dribbled over her chin, but her tongue caught it. She noticed my watching and smiled. She carefully picked up the eclair and slid it into her mouth, biting off the end. After a heavy sigh, she dipped it back into the Anglaise and swirled. My neck tingled, and my ears stung. As she continued her ritual, I sucked in a deep breath and sipped some water. By the time she finished, I was exhausted.

A final, slow lick and she finished.

The waiter appeared, "May I get you something else: coffee? Aperitif perhaps?"

"Yeah," I answered. "Where's the men's room?"

Diana said, "Don't be long, James. We should hurry to get home."

On the interstate as we reached West Virginia, a bank of dark clouds rolled in from the west. By the time we reached Morgantown, a light rain was falling in the darkened town. We saw lightning and heard thunder as the rain increased and then began to pound, and she steered through sheets of rain, wipers moving furiously. At her house, tree limbs littered the yard and sidewalk. Smaller branches twisted in the darkened sky. Diana parked in front of the house, rain pouring off the roof.

"We have to hurry!" she called out. "Quick, dash!"

Like we had been swimming across a pond, we splashed onto her porch. We shook like dogs and stomped our feet.

I began to shiver. "Hurry!" I said as she struggled with the lock.

We were met with darkness before she got to the floor lamp, just before a sharp thunder clap. The lamp flickered on.

"Here," she said. "We need to get out of these clothes."

"But I have nothing to change into."

"We'll figure something out." She unbuttoned my shirt. "You'll have to get out of these pants now."

Reluctant, I unzipped my damp cords. "Don't look. I need a towel or something."

"I'll get something while you undress." She turned toward the hallway.

"Thanks."

She brought towels, a quilt, and a handful of T-shirts. "This'll keep you warm. I'll drape your clothes over a wooden rack. By the way, James, you look cute."

"I feel cold. Goose bumps."

She threw a towel at me and turned away, pulling off the wet blouse. She dried her hair, leaning side to side, and then wrapped the towel around her waist, leaving her bare breasts exposed.

Looking good, I thought.

She scrambled for the shirt, and the towel fell.

Her body fully exposed. What's wrong with me. She showed everything, and it didn't arouse me.

The lamp flickered again. "Maybe you should switch on another one."

"I'm afraid to. Old-fashioned fuse system."

I began to warm and shifted under the quilt. Except for the lightning still crackling, complete darkness covered the house. I said, "Pretty big place for just one person."

"My roommates moved out last month—a graduate student and her husband movin' in next month."

"And you're moving back to Pittsburgh?"

"I'm excited," she said, "living with my family again and law school."

Her exuberance moved me. Her eyes brightened over a broad smile. I touched her arm. "I admire you."

"So, James, what are your plans for the future?"

"College, for sure."

"Any idea for a major?"

"Not sure. Just a good education."

"Where would you like to go to school?"

"Somewhere down South where it's warm!"

The lamp flickered again. I let go of her arm. "You know, Diana, I realize I have lived a sheltered life. When I saw the ocean for the first time, it opened my soul."

"You really are a country boy."

"Yeah. All I ever knew was them mountains. Traipsin' through the woods, pickin' berries, and huntin'. That was my world. Now…"

"Let's get more comfortable," Diana said. "I'm dry and warm, and I have some huckleberry wine we can share."

"I don't think I can get home in this weather."

Diana rose for the kitchen. "You can stay here."

"Nice."

"On a night like this," she said, "I don't want to be alone."

We sat quietly then, sipping the wine and hearing the storm pounding the roof. I felt the warmth of the wine and loosened my hold on the quilt. "You think my clothes are dry now?"

"Underwear, maybe," she said. "I'll get them for you."

After a heavy sigh, my eyes slowly closed, though I was trying to fight it. Diana returned with my underpants and a large T-shirt. I noticed her red panties. She hadn't bothered with a bra, and her breasts bounced. She looked down at me.

"Why don't we move to the bed? I'm getting sleepy, too."

"The wine," I mumbled. "I could do with a soft mattress."

We lay on our backs spread-eagled at first under the soft warmth, under the covers of sheets and a blanket. We sighed in unison.

"It's been quite a day," she said. "I enjoyed it."

"I did, too. Except for the combat with that lobster."

She chuckled and tapped my shoulder. "Country boy."

In the darkness, the welcome feeling of peace came over us. I curled up, and she rolled over, putting her arm around me, perfectly soft against my chest. and we fell asleep.

🌳

When Diana dropped me off the next day, she decided to stay awhile. I introduced her to my parents, who were delighted to meet her, my mother especially, welcoming her with open arms. I saw how my mother responded when Diana asked, "What smells so good?"

"That's the Dutch potato filling."

"Oh-h-h!"

"It's Pennsylvania Dutch."

"Mmmm, something else?"

"Rhubarb pie."

Diana smiled. "I've only had rhubarb pie store-bought and have never had potatoes like that."

"Would you like to join us? We eat about two."

"Oh, I wouldn't want to impose!"

"But you're Jimmy's friend! Please sit down with us!"

After Diana excused herself for the bathroom, Mother smiled at me. "A nice girl, Jimmy. Those eyes, green as the Cheat."

"I like her. She's been great company."

"What are your plans now?"

"Ride out the next week and a half. Have fun before…"

My mother's face fell.

I touched her shoulder. "Don't worry, Ma. I'll be safe there. All I'll be doing is running around and writing stories. I won't even carry a gun no more."

"You're a good boy, Jimmy. You deserve a better life than that!"

"I intend to do just that. I'll use the GI Bill for college when I get back."

"I'll be so proud!"

Diana returned. "I want to thank you, Mrs. Flaherty. You've been so gracious."

"Oh, honey, you're always welcome! Why don't you and Jimmy go out to the garden and bring in tomatoes and corn."

I led her back to a large garden where the leaves still bore the drops of last night's rain. Stepping gingerly around the mud, we each carried a basket and picked off a few ripe tomatoes. The ears of corn snapped off easily, and soon the two baskets were full. On the way back to the house, we sat on the old bench under the cherry tree and husked the corn.

"This smells so good! Nothing like fresh from the garden." She took a smaller tomato and gently bit into it.

"Jimmy. Last night"—she put her hand on my forearm—"I woke up with my arm around your chest." She squeezed. "Your muscle is so hard!"

I glanced at her. "You enjoy?"

"Very much. You're thin, but your muscles are…"

"Well, you can touch them anytime you like."

She laughed and pushed my shoulder. Then she picked up another ear of corn.

🌳

Back in the kitchen with the baskets of tomatoes and husked corn, Diana moved around alongside my mother. "What can I do to help?" Her hand was on Mother's shoulder.

"Oh, sweetheart, thank you! You could start cutting the corn off the cobs. I'm going to add it to the limas."

"Succotash! I love succotash!"

"Well, you're really going to love it fresh! With some cornbread and potatoes to go with the meat, OK?"

"What kind of meat?"

"Rabbit."

"I never ate rabbit before."

"You'll love it," she continued. "We'll season some flour and dredge the rabbit pieces in it. Here, you try."

Diana followed and drew the meat through the flour and then onto the waiting platter. With the oil heating up in the black frying pan, Mother added, "When ya throw in a tiny bit of water and it splatters, it's hot enough."

She let Diana fry up all the rabbit and then called in me and Dad.

We sat around the table, and Dad asked, as usual, for the horseradish. Mother served Diana first. "Go ahead and start. Don't wait on us, 'cause you're the honored guest!" She wiped her hands on her apron and went back to the kitchen for the horseradish.

She returned as we unfolded napkins.

"Diana," I said, noticing her knife and fork, "just eat it with your fingers, like chicken."

We ate quietly at first. Then I offered, "Diana's going to law school this fall."

"That right?"

"And, Dad, she's going into labor law."

"We could sure use more of them! Our union lawyer's retired. We're lookin' for a replacement."

"Why labor law?" Mother asked.

"My mother is a lawyer, and she's worked with labor."

"Following in her footsteps." I said.

"Wow!" Mother smiled. "Not only beautiful but smart too! I envy you, girl."

For the first time, I saw Diana blush. I touched her wrist. "How do you like the food?"

"Delicious! Especially the rabbit and potatoes. I've never had them this way."

"One of my favorites. Can we get you anything else?"

"Oh, goodness, no! I'm getting so full."

"How about a small piece of pie with some ice cream?"

"Let's go out on the porch." I rose and took her elbow.

"You two run along." Dad creaked up from the table. "I'm gonna turn on the ball game."

On the glider, the cushions were soft, and we relaxed in a cool breeze. The sunlight dappled through the cherry tree, and we listened to the rustling of the mountain sounds. A catbird mewed from the thicket, and crows cawed from the distant sky. I thought of…the fall colors to return and the crisp winter air; in my other world, there were only two seasons: rainy and dry. There, I would wear the same clothes all year. I was reminded then of my next job: traveling and writing stories on Nixon's pacification/Vietnamization policy. Why they picked me was a mystery, but I looked forward to the new job—another adventure, more learning, new possibilities? Anyway, eight more months and then freedom, and I would have completed my latest obligation. My adult life had been spent over there. I felt a nudge on my shoulder.

"James, were you daydreaming?"

"Yes, sorry!"

"I'd like to tell you something." She took a deep breath. "I had another great day today. Thank you."

"Me too. I'll sure miss you when I leave."

Diana closed her eyes and whispered, "James Flaherty, I'm going to miss you, too."

"Not for another week."

"A week. It'll seem like a day."

I kissed her forehead. "My folks like you."

"I like them. I think my parents would like your parents."

I looked at her.

She smiled. "If only…C'mon, I better go now."

We stepped back into the living room, where my dad sat in his easy chair listening to the radio. Mother was on the sofa.

"Mr. and Mrs. Flaherty, thank you so much for the delicious meal and your hospitality."

"You're welcome, dear. Come visit us anytime you'd like and get away from the city. You're always welcome!"

Diana bent over and kissed my mother's cheek. She waved to my father. I walked her to the car.

"Y'know," I said, "there's one more thing I like to do that I've missed for years."

"Yes?"

"Racetrack. I'd love to go again. Have you ever?"

"No, but it sounds fun."

"I have some things to do around here, but how about day after tomorrow? Three o'clock?"

She smiled. "That'll be fine. Your car or mine?"

"You oughta hang on to her," Mother was saying the next morning. I'd been pulling weeds and throwing them in a pile near the corn stalks. I grabbed the hoe for some more digging when she approached. "She's honest. And obvious she likes you."

"I like her." I bent down to untangle a root. "We get along."

Again, I felt that pang of guilt, the way I had been treating my parents these past three years. They had to be living in terror that their son could be in grave danger. After my first tour of duty in Vietnam, I came home to them but disappeared and melted into the countryside without a word. Adventure. An anonymous, roving wanderer in search of nothing more than life experience. I traveled into the wilderness of new ideas and new people but was home in a country that no longer felt like my home—driven, always driven, and avoiding suspicious people, avoiding the ubiquitous Jesus freaks with their leather sandals and those others who were suspicious of me. Finally, relying on the kindness of some who could trust a stranger, I reached San Francisco as a pauper and lived in and on Broadway for handouts until I ran out of hope and options. Penniless, I reupped in the army for three years; a short burst and just three days after that, I resurfaced in Vietnam again. No one at home knew. Once again I was one of the unwilling led by the incompetent to do the unnecessary.

Now, as I stood before my mother, she was again encouraging me. Diana had indeed become special. We enjoyed each other's company and were getting to know one another. We had adventures yet in front of us, but we had little time.

"Yeah, Ma, she sure is special. But I don't think any more will come of it. I'll be gone, and we'll each move on with our lives."

"A pity."

"I know, Ma." Looking toward the house, I said, "I'll help Dad with the porch tomorrow, and then Diana and I are goin' to the track up in Chester."

Chapter 5

Sixteen days

We arrived at the racetrack early the next evening. The narrow roads to Weirton hadn't hindered the old Volkswagen, and parking was easy. After a short walk, I bought the blue ad-tab before entering the gate, where we joined with the gathering crowd. We saw the slickers with fedoras and shades deliberating over the program and young couples with starry-eyed expectations aimlessly meandering.

"Let's get a greasy hamburger," I said, "and some soggy fries."

"You make it sound so palatable!"

"A couple of 3.2 drafts would also do well."

"Yum!" She rolled her eyes.

"You have to get into the spirit here! This is the racetrack, the best place to indulge and throw your money away."

"Aren't you supposed to win money?"

"Maybe, maybe not. I leave that to the high rollers. Those with gambling problems. We're just here for fun."

"You're so positive!"

I added, "By the way, I like the way you look. Mean Jewish girl, you're not that mean, are you?"

"Could be." She winked.

"I bet Dwight likes that shirt."

"You're going to find out how mean I can be! C'mon! You'll grovel in grease for that."

Back from concessions, I sipped beer. "Look over the program. See if you can pick some winners. I'll cross-reference the ad-tab."

"What's the ad-tab?"

Diana fingered down the first race roster. "Here, I like this one, Buddy Blue."

"That's twelve to one. You might want to pick another."

She made a stern face. "I pick Buddy Blue!"

"Why, mean Jewish girl."

She slapped my wrist and giggled. "You're eyes are blue and its my favorite color. So play it, or I'll show you how mean I can be. She laughed outright and brushed my cheeks with both hands.

"OK, OK. I'll go to the two-dollar window."

When I reached the window, the horse's odds had jumped to twenty-four to one. I shook my head and placed the bet. "Goodbye, my money."

I returned to her, and we crossed to the infield, where the bright lights illuminated the dusk. As the horses were led into the starting gate, we saw Buddy Blue kicking and shaking his head. The jockey struggled with the reins.

"Is that a good sign?" Her face was quizzical.

No, I thought. "Maybe, we'll see."

The bell rang, and the horses left the gate, Buddy Blue leaping out in front. They thundered to the first turn as his lead evaporated into the pack. They watched as the horse fell further behind, slowing to a lumber around the clubhouse turn. I thought about tearing up the ticket and tossing it when Buddy Blue caught second wind and began gaining on the others, gaining, and passing them one by one down the stretch, to cheering and our amazement, and won!

Diana, eyes wide, asked, "What happened?"

"We won! I'll go get two more beers. Study that program while I collect our money." I returned with forty-eight dollars and two drafts. Diana was studying the program.

Her eyes lit up and her finger stopped on a name. I looked closer.

"Arnold's Choice."

"Strange."

"My brother's name is Arnold! He's a successful contractor in Saint Louis, a sure winner!"

"Eight to one, OK, better. Do you know what I think?"

"Hmm?"

"Across the board."

"What's that?"

"First, second, and third place. We put two dollars across the board." She viewed the program. "I don't see it here."

"So Arnold comes in first, second, or third, then the ticket pays."

"He's gonna win!"

"Then we win all three bets. Here, drink this. I'm going to the two-dollar window."

The track was crowded now; lines had formed at the two-dollar windows. I dashed up and down for an opening as people were unhurriedly placing bets, often more than one. I gave up and sped to the open ten-dollar window. "Number six across."

Back with Diana, I said, "I hope Arnold at least comes in third."

"Why third? He's gonna win!"

"I had to go to the ten-dollar window."

We decided to stay inside and listen to the race over the loudspeaker. The horses left the gate, and the announcer singsonged their names as they galloped but not Arnold's. Tense, Diana gripped my arm and listened. I was beginning to lose hope, thinking about the lost ten dollars, when the name *Arnold's Choice* came over the din. They were coming down the stretch, Arnold's Choice gaining with every stride, the cheering deafening. "Arnold's Choice, the winner!"

Diana screamed and hugged me. I hugged her.

"You're somethin'." I kissed her cheek and went to collect.

One hundred, sixty-seven dollars richer, we decided to skip the third race. Going over the fourth race line-up, she said, "I don't see anything catching my eye, but check this out." She was pointing to the fifth race, her finger on an entry, "Rapscallion."

"What's that?"

"From my favorite book! Huck Finn tried to dissuade the reader from seeing him as a 'rapscallion.'"

"What's it mean?"

"A mischievous person."

"Charming!"

"And look at this. The silks are green."

"To match your eyes mean girl. We have thirty minutes till post time for the fifth. Why don't we get some air?"

We ambled through the gates to the concourse outside where cool air met us. The noise from the crowd and the announcer was quieter there, and we enjoyed the sounds of the next race from a distance. We recalled to each other, laughing, the previous days' activities and predicaments. I guided her toward the first-turn area where we could see the lights and bright colors of the track's visitors. She clasped my hand, and we strolled along until I put my arm over her shoulder and kissed her cheek. Surprisingly, she kissed my lips. I withdrew.

"That was bold."

"I felt like it!"

"Well, I did like it." It was a kiss I'd missed. Over the years, I'd forgotten that feeling. A true kiss; filled with a passion that had been missing.

"So did I! Jimmy, I'd been working hard my senior year and concentrating so hard to get into law school, I just wasn't having any fun at all. With you, I am. Thank you!"

"I should be thanking you. Without you, my leave would be so boring."

"But so short! I wish it were longer, at least up to when I start at Duquesne."

"What's short is just having eight more months; then I'll be a civilian again."

"But then you'll be living down South." She sighed.

"Yeah, I'll have to, and believe me, I know what boring is!" I smiled.

"Thank you." She squeezed my arm. "Now let's get back to Rapscallion."

We decided to bet the horse across the board at the fifty-dollar window. After looking over the program, we determined there were no more entries that stood out.

Rapscallion ran a good race but faded in the stretch, finishing fourth. For the first time that evening, I tore a ticket in half.

The deepening darkness outside made the concourse lights seem brighter, and Diana's eyes glistened with them. Looking up to mine, she said, "I think I'd like to go home now."

"But aren't you havin' fun?"

"Sure, but I'd rather be alone with you." She slid her hand down my arm. "You kissed me, and I liked it. I'd like more."

Stunned, I stepped away. "But that's not what we're supposed to be doing."

"What are we supposed to be doing?"

"Havin' fun, doin' things. Not sex."

She wrinkled into a smile. "Whoever said anything about sex? I just want to get to know you better, OK?"

"Let's go then."

Diana left two small lamps on in the living room where we settled in and sat together on the large sofa. She crossed a leg over me and squeezed my hand. "You are confusing me. You enjoy our time together but in only a platonic way. Don't you ever get aroused?"

"Sometimes, sure. You're beautiful. How can I not notice?"

She stroked my cheek and then turned and kissed me, which led to my arms around her, lingering, feeling the heat of her back. She took my hand and led it inside her blouse. I cupped the roundness of her breast, nipple between fingers, and she kissed my neck, then my ears, and then lowered her hand to my crotch, but there was nothing. She drew back.

"You're a cold man, James Flaherty."

"I don't agree," I protested. "There's just more to it."

"I guess I can't figure you out."

"Then don't try. It might not be what you think."

She rested under my shoulder and breathed quietly.

I stroked her hair. "You don't get me, and I…don't understand myself; I have a hard time relating. I get tongue-tied, and I…I feel… stupefied."

"Numb, I think. I heard of that. Sometimes a traumatized person shuts down."

"I don't know much about psychology, but I think you're right. Being with you has been great. I've been doing what I like, and you're a wonderful companion. Loafing together has been fun, but for some reason, I can't go beyond this. Understand?"

She gently smiled. "Maybe we should have some space. We can still do things, just not every day."

"Maybe, but I'm gettin' short. Only a couple of weeks left now, and I'd like to divide my time between you and my family."

"Fine." She smiled, and it was then I realized just how beautiful Diana was.

Maybe I should have tried her right then—maybe she'd help me feel better about myself—but for now, I was happy with our relationship. I kissed her cheek. "May I return three days from now?"

"Why so long?" She kissed my forehead, and I rose from her and let myself out.

Chapter 6

Twelve days

I was in a comfortable routine, those two weeks. Her charm grew on me, and it was as if the girl I was getting to know was actually different each time I saw her.

On the last Sunday of my leave, we sat together on a log bench atop Cooper Rock, surrounded by mountain laurel, looking over the Cheat River Gorge and the blue-green mountains with their shadowy folds and steep slopes. Her loose hair blew lightly across her face. She wore jeans and a white T-shirt under her jungle shirt.

She sighed. "Of all the places I've ever been, this is the most tranquil."

"I used to come here all the time growing up, but I never really appreciated it. Until now."

"Now," she said in a strange tone of finality. She sucked in a deep breath. She tucked her sneakered feet onto the bench, raised one knee, rested her face on it, and looked at me. "All this time we've been seeing each other it's been great, the driving, the races, the dinners and lunches, lounging around on the porch. It's not like you haven't had opportunities, yet you never, you know, tried anything. Am I to take it then I'm not attractive to you?"

"Of course you're attractive, Diana! I think you're beautiful!"

She breathed deeply. "I could consider that an insult."

"That I think you're beautiful?"

"Don't act silly."

"What do you want me to say? You want me to kiss you?" A strand floated onto my face, and I brushed it away and kissed her cheek and then her ear. "There," I whispered. "Is that what you want?"

She pulled away. "The question is, James, what do *you* want?"

"Don't talk anymore. Just let me kiss you."

"C'mon, I'm trying to be serious."

"So am I. OK, so what'll it be?" I leaned away. "I don't know, except I enjoy being with you. I'm sorry if that insults you."

She took my shoulders and closed in, raising her face to mine. Our lips met as I saw through tears. I closed my eyes as we touched each other in embrace, my arms around her back, hands in the warmth of her neck. Slowly, with deep breaths, we parted. A quick breeze swept up from the gorge and lifted her hair around my fingers, and I was aware of my heart suddenly racing as it did during the most ferocious fighting I'd experienced. It was a strange parallel, that loving and killing would both cause the same reaction in the heart. There was, though, the difference in the feeling of peace afterward, the difference between survival and bliss.

Suddenly aware, I said, "You know, I grew up in a place of Friday night dances, quarts of beer, and routine fights outside the dance hall. The most important topic on girls' minds there was the choice of husband and the latest gossip, usually about who had gained a 'reputation.' I never knew a girl who was politically active, who had a cause beyond making herself available to a potential mate. And no girl has ever asked me the question you just asked. Things have really changed."

She faced me. "Only a few more days together. A month ago, no one could have told me that this would ever happen, not me! It's been fast, maybe too fast, but I've loved every minute I've spent with you."

"It's going to be hard to leave." I looked away. "I need to help my folks some more at home before I go. But maybe..." I turned back to her. "I could come back Wednesday?"

"Come back as early as you can," she answered.

Chapter 7

Eight days

I spent the next two days with my mother and father. I organized the few things I'd brought with me and packed my gear for the end of my leave. As I helped with the garden, plants, and shrubs my folks kept around the house, I told them as much as I could about the coming year, assuring them that I'd be perfectly safe. They had never understood what motivated me to return to Nam after my first tour, nor why I had disappeared like I did when I roamed the countryside until I ended up in California, where I had reenlisted. I had never told them about those times, and they never asked. They seemed happy to have me home, even though they hadn't seen much of me. About what I was doing with my time, they were careful not to ask either; they only knew I would be leaving in a few days.

In the dark, Tuesday night, I sat on the back porch, smelling the grass I had cut that afternoon. I was counting the hours.

🌳

The next morning, her house was cool and dark when she opened the door. She hugged me and told me she was working on breakfast. After scrambled eggs, toast with jelly, tea, and cut orange slices, I sat at the table as she tended to the kitchen and cleaned up. From the front room, an occasional car whispered by outside. Streaks of eastern sunlight revealed floating dust particles and a thin film on the panes. Birds chattered in the sycamores.

She finally came to me, and I stood. She put her hands on my shoulders.

"James, we have only two days," she said softly and distinctly, "and two nights left." The hollow of her throat fluttered, "I want to spend them here with you." She raised herself up and kissed me. Then she drew away. "Let's go upstairs."

Her bedroom was dark with the morning chill. The heavy boughs of the trees shaded the screened windows. The large, high-mattressed bed was already arranged with the covers folded back, and the dark oak headboard reached nearly to the ceiling, giving me the impression that on the bed we would be secluded from the whole world.

When she took my hand, I could feel the nervousness we both felt. We pressed together and kissed, my heart pounding against her, and though chilled, I began to sweat. Her lips were moist with perspiration.

We slowly undressed each other, and then I felt her skin hot against mine as we fell onto the bed. I covered her and kissed her, my hands shaking, and then she spread her legs and raised her hips. She gasped when I penetrated her, and quickly, too quickly, it was over.

We lay side by side. I put my arm around her and whispered, "Sorry."

"Sorry?"

"I didn't mean to…for it to be so fast."

She smiled. "I was so worried. I wanted it to be perfect." She gazed at the cracked pale-green ceiling and sighed with content. "I guess a thing like this can't be planned."

"You surprised me."

"Told you before I was full of surprises." She smiled.

For the next two days, our lovemaking reached beyond either's imaginable limit.

We roamed the house half-dressed, she in her jungle shirt and I in a pair of cutoff shorts with no underwear. Sometimes we dressed to go onto the front porch and sit on the glider; other times, we would go onto the screened landing beside the kitchen and sit in the afternoon sun. We snacked on what she had in the kitchen and drank wine, a glass here and there. We even attended to small chores, like taking out the trash, straightening up, and sweeping.

We made love whenever we were moved. Once while sitting in the kitchen, I was watching Diana sweep the floor when she bent over to gather up the dustpan. I saw the soft hair under the long tails of her shirt, and aroused, I went to her, braced her against the cabinet, held her hips, and took her quickly. Another time as I sat on the sofa listening to the stereo, she emerged from the kitchen, naked. She stepped onto the couch and stood over me, her hands on her hips. She gyrated and lowered herself over my face, and I responded with my tongue until she arched and moaned. We lay on the rug, sometimes pillows and blankets, fondling each other with moist kisses. Once she said, "Wait right here," and returned from the kitchen with a jar of peanut butter and another of grape jelly. Giggling, she stroked it onto my stomach, thighs, and hardening penis and swore she would eat it all…and did. Soon after, I wanted her again, but propped up with a couch pillow, her hips weren't high enough, so I went to the bookshelf and found two books that fit perfectly: *A Brief Survey of Western Civilization* and a thin copy of the Tao Te Ching. On my knees, I then lifted her thighs and pulled her to me, turning her laughter into a squeal and then heavy breathing.

"I guess I have been put on a pedestal." She laughed over a glass of wine afterward.

"But just think about it," I said, "we've found our place in history, proving wrong the idea that the twain shall never meet!"

We enjoyed an afternoon nap, while still penetrated after coupling, as cicadas sawed away outside.

The last evening, as we lay together, she kissed me and said softly, "Why don't we drive to Jersey early in the morning instead of you flying?"

Chapter 8

Two days

We woke before dawn the next morning and gathered our things. We took a shower together, which led to more lovemaking, before we dressed and headed out in the dark. Diana wore a pair of khaki shorts, a sweatshirt, and high-topped hiking boots over thick socks pulled well up her calves. No sooner had we crossed the Cheat River Bridge than I swelled with another erection. As if the past two days were not enough, I was astonished, I couldn't get enough of her.

We pulled into the dirt driveway beside my house just as sunlight crept through the grape trellis. While I collected my khaki uniform, one pair of jungle fatigues, my leave orders, and toiletries, Diana chatted with my folks. I could see in my mother's eyes the same fear as when I first went to Vietnam four years earlier. It made me feel cruel, knowing she sensed the change in me, the perceptions and feelings that had guided me to this bizarre return to the war zone.

Before we left, I hugged her tightly as I told her I would be perfectly safe this time and that in less than a year, I'd be back with them. I sensed, though, from her silence that she was afraid of losing forever a son. My father, for his part, hid his feelings as he usually did, nodding and smiling as Diana and I drove away.

We were on our way then silently, almost gloomily. I drove her car along the narrow country road following the base of the Laurel Highlands, over hills of clover and tall green corn stalks, and past quiet towns whose names ended in "Furnace," as if the old coke ovens still flared inside. We went through Connellsville and Mount Pleasant before winding around through Donegal to the Pennsylvania Turnpike.

Sailing east on the super highway, we crossed the highlands and more farmland valleys glistening in the morning sun. She suddenly laughed. "You know, I just had a strange thought. A month ago, nobody would've told me I'd be doing this, have done what we've been doing! It's put the whole rest of the world far away."

"I know what you mean. I haven't thought about Nam until today."

In silence, we climbed the Alleghenies. Through the open windows, the fragrance of wild grape blossoms wafted in. At noon, we found a roadside picnic table and stopped for the lunch she had packed. After eating, we took a short walk into the woods where we kissed and held each other. We soon found ourselves half-naked in the grip of passion.

"I'll never forget you, what we've shared these past two weeks. Especially the last three days," I felt her tears on my chest. "Oh, James, I loved you! That's something you can always know."

Later, after we had dressed, her words echoed in my head. "But do you love me now?"

"Even more." She smiled, and we returned to the car, my arm around her waist.

We agreed to leave the turnpike as soon as we could for the picturesque Route 30 running parallel. After stopping for gas at a Phillips 66, back on the road, she put her hand gently on my arm. "I'm so grateful for being a woman now, but I'm sorry at the same time."

I paused, not wanting to respond, but after taking a deep breath, I said, "I love you."

It was then, on the highway, that I suddenly thought: *I don't want to go back!*

"You know, it's not over yet," I said. "I wish it would never end!"

I had already served for three years there, I thought. I should have no trouble getting out at this point.

"Do you really want it not to end?" I asked.

Confusion crossed her face.

Only a little more than a year, I thought. Surely they'd take that into consideration. "I mean, if I got out of the army and came back."

"Oh, James, don't be silly! Out?"

"Yeah, out. Just like that!" And, I thought, there are the decorations I'd earned. They'd have to consider those, too.

"You're not making any sense."

"It makes all kinds of sense, don't you see?"

Diana folded her arms and crossed her legs toward the door. I could see her tight-lipped expression.

"Don't you want me to come back?"

She stared away from me out the window. Uncrossing her legs, she sighed and smoothed the hair away from her eyes. "James, why don't we get off this subject once and for all? Today is what counts, so let's take it for all it's worth for both of us and forget about what lies ahead." She turned and faced me. "Agreed?"

I longed for that secluded house of hers, the privacy and intimacy we shared there, shielded behind the old trees buzzing with cicadas. In the cool darkness, we, two from different backgrounds and situations, shed our inhibitions and constraints. Having met in lucky confusion, we had grown on each other to the point that an uncommon fusion of simple humanity had taken over. Perhaps that was all there was to it; by the end of the day, it would be over, but despite what I knew, the hope kept stirring in my mind that I could change the ending.

"Yeah," I finally said. "Agreed."

With that, we made our way down Route 30, listening to the radio, sometimes singing along. The sun arced behind us, beginning its long summer descent. Fast-moving cloud fluffs sent shadows across fields, skimming the red barns and neat, deep-green fields.

Near the town of York, the husky, golden-brown leaves of burley tobacco curling open appeared to drink in the rays of the sunlight. Across the Susquehanna in Lancaster County, the corn rose taller and greener, and we began to see bearded men and bonneted women in wagons pulled by trotting horses. Boys with bowl haircuts and drab gray pants supported by large suspenders over white shirts stole glances at the passing cars, while the young girls stared ahead, the bonnets they wore permitting no wandering eyes.

Diana and I marveled at them, musing aloud what it would be like to live in such a simple manner. Those thoughts left us when we entered the town of Intercourse, which brought from us both sly smiles. We pulled into the parking lot of a small, red-bricked inn that was crowded with cars bearing license plates from around the country.

"Let's see if there are any rooms available," I said. "It's so beautiful and serene here; it'd be a shame to pass right through."

"But don't you have to report?"

"Aww, it doesn't matter if I'm a little late. They don't care in those processing centers. Besides, this way you won't have to drive back at night."

We were in luck: there was a tiny room on the second floor, far to one end of the place. The woman apologized for the cramped space but explained the room had been used in the off-season for storage. The hardwood floor reflected the sunlight streaming through the small paned window, and a large oval rag rug of red, blue, and green covered the center of the floor. In the corner below the slanted ceiling was a four-poster bed with a quilted spread and goose-down pillows fluffed at the head.

"This is adorable," Diana breathed.

"Charming," I replied to agree and looked into the tiny bathroom, which contained a shower stall barely large enough for one person and an old ornately plumbed sink and commode. "Simply charming."

She came up behind me, wrapped her arms around my chest, and leaned her head into my back. "C'mon, James. Where's your sense of adventure?"

"I woulda thought," I said, gesturing to the sink, "we'd see one of those pitchers and washbasins instead of that."

I turned to her, and she stood on her toes, her arms around my neck. Quietly she looked into my eyes and then kissed my lips gently. She smoothed my mustache with her finger before kissing me again. Her arms slid down around my waist and held tightly, her head resting against my chest with a sigh.

"This is what I need most of all. I love the smell of you, James, the hardness of your muscles, and the rasp in your voice, and your heart beating."

My arms around her, I squeezed gently. She felt the tension of my muscles and could hear and feel my quickening heartbeat.

"I love you," she whispered.

"You've been good for me, so good."

Tears filled her eyes as a shudder passed over her. I tenderly rubbed her back and neck and then raised her chin and kissed her forehead and then her neck. Her head tilted back as she sucked in a tiny breath. When she kissed my neck, my pulse seemed to pass through her in rhythm with her own. She held her lips there feeling the strong vibrations, opening herself for my pulse and heartbeat against her breast. It was like the first time our lips met, tenderly, deeply.

As if floating on air, we felt the mattress beneath us. Time slowed down as it had in the past three days, as we reached a higher plane, the deep sensual essence of becoming one. My naked body pressed against her, arousing the familiar instinct; her opening and rising for me had become the natural anticipation. She received me with the heart of love, much more deeply penetrated, feeling the fusion into oneness. My kiss, my embrace, and soft, slow strokes reached her soul. Time had no measure in that little room as my love spilled into her. The flow fused with her own, forging a love that could not escape.

We lay there dreamily, exhausted and damp with love. Like returning consciousness, the mundane sounds and smells of the evening returned: a child yelled, calling someone in for supper and trees rustled leaves in the faint breeze, which carried to us the smell of newly mown hay through the lace curtains. Diana remembered the scents of Queen Anne's lace and the purple-throated Indian tobacco of earlier in the day.

"James."

My chest rose and fell. I turned my head to her, cheeks flushed.

"Do you think we just created life?" she continued.

"I don't know."

"I feel…wonderful."

I stroked her face and then her hair. She could see the flush of my face, kissed me, and said softly, "Maybe we should get something to eat."

"OK, in a few more minutes."

We kissed again, and the lace softly danced across our naked bodies in the gathering dusk.

A full moon illuminated the darkness at 4:00 a.m. as we quietly checked out and slipped away. We got back on the turnpike to get through Philadelphia and cross the oily Delaware crowded with naval and commercial ships. Into the streets of Camden we passed as the sun peeked over the horizon. We continued on into rural New Jersey, just seventy miles from Fort Dix.

We reached Wrightstown after a quiet drive through the pine forests and stopped at the Main Street ice cream shop. I got a coffee, and Diana went to the counter for a double cone. I felt that strong resistance in her returning as when we first met three weeks earlier. She seemed to go into herself, and it was as though she was back in that doorway, the heavy oak door just cracked open, her green eyes shy in the semidarkness. Both of us weary and sad with anticipation, we had barely spoken when she asked only to drop me off quickly so she could make it back to Pittsburgh that evening.

Her eyes downcast over the ice cream cone, I drove onto the base through the gate, past the spit-shined MP guards, and on, passing rows of yellow wooden barracks, columns of marching troops, and olive-drab trucks rumbling by. She never looked up. Arriving, I parked in front of HQ and unloaded my bag from the trunk. Diana got out, walked around the front of her car to the driver's side, and settled herself behind the wheel. I shouldered my bag and closed the trunk. I stepped to the window.

"Will you be all right?"

She nodded slightly.

"I mean driving alone?"

Another slight nod.

"I'll call you tonight. Or maybe you can call me here. You know, let me know you made it all right?"

"There's no need," she said softly. "I'll be fine."

I waited. She stared out the windshield, and then without looking at me, she handed me the ice cream cone and took the wheel.

"Take care of yourself," she said. "Please."

She drove away. I held the melting cone as I watched her leaving. I watched her turn left and then drive out of sight. No wave. No kiss, just "Take care of yourself" and "Please."

I reported to the Ninetieth Replacement Company. The captain in command had served as a helicopter pilot, which created a sort of camaraderie between us; I told him my plan to be discharged early.

"Then you're going to be here a long time," he said.

"Why do you say that?"

"Look around you! This is a training base, and not one of them wants to be the last to die in Vietnam. You're not the only one wants to get out."

"Then I'll be in a long line."

"Yeah, well, I wouldn't want to be in that psychiatrist's shoes." The captain looked gaunt.

"Sir, when did you get back from Vietnam?"

"A couple of months ago."

"About as long as I. Did you want this job?"

"I take what the army gives me."

I saw the First Aviation pennant on the wall and the brightly shining wings above it. I wondered how many missions he had flown; it might have been many, and that would explain his nervous presentation. He offered, "Nice chatting with you. I'll get the clerk to find you a bunk."

I chose a lower bunk and settled down for some rest. I could hear the marching of trainee boots in the distance and smelled kerosene through the cracked window. After a short nap, dreaming about Diana, I realized I had to get in touch with her. I went to the nearby orderly room to get directions to the USO and asked the clerk if I could use the typewriter.

He refused. "It's government property."

"It'll be just a few minutes. I type fast. And, hey, I'll even do your morning report tomorrow."

"What's going on in here?" the captain interjected.

"Sir, he wants to use the typewriter."

"Is that true?"

"Sir," I answered, "I need to send a letter to my sweetheart, and I type a hundred words a minute; it won't take me long."

He paused and then looked at the clerk. "Let him use the typewriter."

The clerk handed me an envelope and paper, and I started.

Diana Levin
101 Grace St. Morgantown, WVa

Diana,

I'm still in Ft. Dix, applying for a discharge. I don't know how it will work out, and it could take a long time, but I won't give up until a decision is made. I hope you are well. Did you have a good drive back? I already miss the good times with you. Especially that time in the mountains. I don't like it here. What I've been hearing, I'll probably be back in Vietnam soon, but that's OK. I miss all the places we saw, but I miss you most of all.

I love you, James

In the next week, I spent most of my time in the Day Room and the more plush NCO Club. The Day Room had more to offer, like a pool table and a couple of TVs, but the NCO Club felt like a sanctuary. Replacement soldiers busy at the pool table, destined to be shipped all over the world, spoke of their choice assignments, looking forward to new places. It was useless to get acquainted with any, since they arrived and then left so soon after.

I liked the USO, where the permanent party cadre visited. The soldiers there found a break from their daily duties: cooks, clerks, guards, and electricians from the Signal Corps. A lineman once asked me what it was like in Vietnam, but how could I possibly answer that? He wouldn't have understood even if I had tried to tell him. I was beginning to realize that I was living in two different worlds.

One afternoon, back at the barracks, I was surprised by mail from Diana. I read,

James,

It was so great to hear from you, I thought that you would be long gone by now.

Hang in there, and maybe you'll succeed after all. Guess what? I was accepted to Duquesne law! I was so excited I was beside myself. You might not know how important this is to me, all the study and hard work. I earned this privilege, and I wanted to share with you. I don't have much more to say, except that I love you, James, and good luck.

Diana

Fort Dix became more and more boring and the daily routine oppressive. *When is this going to end?* I felt like I could finally answer the lineman's question: *The Green Machine, just different climates. Nothing different from there to here; we each had clerks, cooks, NCO cadres, and the officer corps. And mess halls.* The thoughts depressed me. I decided to write back to Diana.

Diana,

Congratulations on your acceptance to law school. I wish I were there to help you celebrate. This place is wearing on me. It's like a time-less hole of misery. You don't know how many times I'd like to hold you and kiss you. It's coming to September. You must be preparing for school. Did you move back to Pittsburgh? I'm waiting to be called to the psychiatrist for an early out. It's been too long of a wait, and I'm not too confident. While you are at school, please write, even if it's a short note.

I love you,
James

September 7, I went to the USO to call my mother. It was her birthday. She was worried about my being away from home and wanted to hear about where I had been and when I might return. When I got back to the office, the clerk held up some papers.

"Guess what? You've been ordered to report to a social worker tomorrow."

"Where would I go?"

"Building 100, up on the hill."

"What time?"

"O nine hundred. And good luck."

After chow the next morning, I took a long shower and shaved before setting out for the appointment. Fort Dix was part of the new American army; all along the quarter-mile walk, I saw new brick barracks replacing the old weathered wooden ones from years ago. I wondered how many trainees were housed in these buildings, each unit with its sign reading company and battalion. I guessed each building housed about two hundred. Each building would have had a battalion mess hall, maybe run by a civilian contractor. The new exercise areas had freshly planted grass, and I passed one where a company was doing their rhythmic exercises.

I reached the social workers' office and was told to sit in a chair in the hall. A Spec 5 with red hair and thick glasses emerged. "Spec 5 Flaherty?"

I went through the door being held for me.

"Have a seat," he said, offering the chair in front of the desk. "Let's get started. Do you belong to any religious denomination that objects to war?"

"Well, I am a Unitarian."

The redhead jotted on a yellow pad. "According to your 201, you've already spent more than two years in Vietnam. Why now?"

"Because of those two years in Vietnam, I'm war-weary. I've seen enough, too much shit. It's time for me to return to a normal life, if I even can."

"Your file also reports you've won the Purple Heart, Combat Infantryman badge, and Good Conduct medals."

"Does that help my case?"

"It may. I'll send my report to a clinical psychologist who makes the final determination, but honestly, you don't have the religious background to help you."

"You don't understand. I don't want to go back to that place."

"I'm just doing my job here. I will make some more notes and send it on up."

I came away a bit crushed and felt like my chances were slipping away. Maybe I was wasting my time. When I returned to the Replacement Company's barracks, the captain sat on an empty bunk, dangling his legs.

"Well, how did it pan out? Did you learn anything?"

"I don't know, sir. Everything's so confusing. May I speak to you in private?"

Rising off the bunk, he said, "Come to my office, Flaherty."

A couple of minutes later, he asked, "So what's on your mind?"

I told him the whole story, about my leave and meeting the girl and everything that went on after that. The captain asked, "So you want to get out of the army because of the girl?"

"I'm not sure. Everything's gotten so crazy. Sir, I would like you to give me an opinion."

"Sounds like you're carrying a heavy load, and you need to get rid of it."

"What do you think, sir?"

"I'm not here to tell you what to do, but it seems to me you need to face the end of this chapter in your life and move on. What kind of duty do you have in Nam now?"

"Actually it's a pretty easy job in an information office. All I do is write stories and take photos."

"How much longer do you have to serve there?"

"About eight months."

"And your sweetheart is in law school?"

"Yes, sir."

"Well, that eliminates one option, because, essentially, she's gone."

"Sir, do you think I should put myself on the manifest?"

"I would wait a few days to see what washes out with your appeal."

Two weeks later, I still had heard nothing from the psychologist or the social worker, but a letter arrived.

"Flaherty!" came from the clerk's desk. "Another letter from your sweetheart!"

I took it into the barracks and read,

Dear James,

I was going to tell you I thought I was pregnant, but just lately, I must have miscarried. I thought I had gotten pregnant when we stopped in Intercourse. Remember when I asked you if you thought we had created life? I went to my rabbi for advice. I'm so sorry, James, 'cause that had to be your baby. But on the other hand, it might be a blessing to allow me to continue law school. I still love you, but I think it's over between us. I'm sorry.

Love, Diana

I folded it up, into the envelope, and threw it in the metal trash can; then I went to the orderly room and found the clerk.

"Put me on the next manifest."

"You can't just do that," he protested.

"Yes, I can. Nothing has worked out, and besides, the CO told me to just wait a few days, and it's been much longer."

Next I gathered my things and said goodbye to the captain.

Two days later, I was at McGuire Air Force Base boarding a flight to Vietnam. During the thirteen-hour flight, I considered everything that had happened since I started my leave, and I felt as if I were really on my way home, to the place where I had been for almost all of my adult life.

Brown. Colors faded into brown. The brown of life, the brown of earth. At last I reached home.

About the Author

Born in Pittsburgh, Richard Blaney graduated from the University of South Carolina with a degree in international studies. He is a certified working chef and a serious student of history. He lives with his wife, Ann, in Columbia, South Carolina.

Milton Keynes UK
Ingram Content Group UK Ltd.
UKHW031617231124
451036UK00003B/40